HARRY MILLER'S RUN

For Brendan and Beth
DA

For Nick and Lisa and the boys,
Joshua, Daniel and Matthew
SR

First published 2008 in conjunction with Great North Run Culture

This edition published 2015 by Walker Books Ltd
87 Vauxhall Walk, London SE11 5HJ

2 4 6 8 10 9 7 5 3 1

Text © 2008 David Almond
Illustrations © 2015 Salvatore Rubbino

The right of David Almond and Salvatore Rubbino to be identified as author and illustrator respectively of this work has been asserted by them in accordance with the Copyright, Designs and Patents Act 1988

This book has been typeset in Sabon

Printed in China

British Library Cataloguing in Publication Data:
a catalogue record for this book is available from the British Library

ISBN 978-1-4063-6224-4

www.walker.co.uk

DAVID ALMOND

HARRY MILLER'S RUN

illustrated by
SALVATORE RUBBINO

WALKER
BOOKS

I don't want to go to Harry Miller's. It's Saturday morning. My entry for the Junior Great North Run's just come through the post. I'm already wearing the T-shirt. I'm already imagining belting round the quayside and over the bridges in two weeks' time. I'm imagining all the running kids, the cheering crowds. I'm dreaming of sprinting to the finish line. I phone Jacksie and we end up yelling and laughing at each other. His stuff's come as well. He's number 2594. I'm 2593. We can't believe it. But we say it's fate. We've been best mates for ever. We say we'll meet up straight away and get some training done in Jesmond Dene.

But soon as I put the phone down, Mam's at my shoulder.

"Don't go, Liam," she says.

"Eh?"

"Come with me to Harry's. It's his last day in the house. He'll need a friendly face around."

"But, Mam!"

"Come on, just an hour or two. Just for me."

"But I haven't got time, Mam."

She laughs.

"You're eleven years old. You've got all the time in the world."

So in the end I sigh, phone Jacksie again and put him off till the afternoon, and I slouch down the street with my mam.

Harry's ancient. We've known him for ever. He lives at the end of our street and he was fit as a lop till the heart attack got him. It looked like the end but he was soon fighting back. A few days in intensive care, a couple of weeks in Freeman Hospital, and before we knew it he was back home in Blenkinsop Street. He started tottering around his little front garden on his Zimmer frame, tottering past our window to the Elmfield Social Club. He stood gasping at street corners, grinning at the neighbours, waving at the kids. When he saw me out training, he'd yell, "Gan on, young'n! Keep them pins moving!" And I'd wave and laugh and put a sprint on. "That's reet, lad! Run! There's a wolf at your tail! Run for your life!"

Everybody knows Harry. Everybody loves him. The women in the street take him flasks of tea and sandwiches and plates of dinner. His mates from the club call in with bottles of beer to play cards and dominoes with him. The district nurse visits every day and she's always laughing when she comes out his front door. But one day she found him with a massive bruise on his head after he'd had a fall. One day he was out wandering the street in his stripy pyjamas. It couldn't go on. There was nobody at home to look after him. It was time for him to leave the house, get rid of tons of stuff and move into St Mary's, the new nursing home just off Baker's Lane.

Mam took it on herself to help him clear out. "Poor soul," she said. "How on earth'll he bear up?" But Harry didn't seem to find it hard at all. Out went all his stuff, to charity shops and fetes and the town dump: pots and pans, dishes, tables and chairs, clothes, a radio, an ancient TV.

"What are they?" he said. "Nowt but things. Hoy them oot!"

He just laughed about it all.

"I'll not need much in the place where I'm gannin'. And for the place past that, I'll not need nowt at all."

We walk down the street to Harry's. Mam lets us in with
a key. By now, just about everything's gone. The floors are
bare. There're no curtains at the windows. He's sitting in
the front room in a great big armchair with a box full of
papers on his lap and the Zimmer frame standing in front
of him. There's a little table with boxes of tablets on it.
He looks all dreamy but he manages to grin.

"How do, petal," he says.

"How do, Harry."

Mam bends down and kisses him. She pushes some
hair back from his brow. She says has he washed this
morning, has he brushed his teeth, has he had breakfast,
has he...

"Aye," he says. "Aye, hinny, aye."

He stares at me like he's staring from a million miles away.

"It's the little runner," he says at last.

"Aye, Mr Miller."

He reaches out and touches the T-shirt. His hand's all frail an' trembly.

"Great North Run?" he says.

"Aye, Mr Miller."

"I done that."

"Did you really, Harry?" says Mam. "And when was that?"

He reaches towards me again.

"How old are ye, son?"

"Eleven."

"That was when I done it. When I was eleven."

Mam smiles sadly at me.

"Must've been great," she says.

"It was bliddy marvellous, pet."

He closes his eyes. Mam lifts the box from his lap. It looks like he might be dropping off to sleep, but he jumps up to his feet and grabs the Zimmer frame. He leans forward like he's ready to run.

"It's the final sprint!" he says.

He giggles and drops back into the chair.

"Tek nae notice, son," he says. "I'm just a daft old maddled gadgie."

He looks at the box.

"Them'll need to be gone through," he says. "Ye'll help us, hinny?"

"Course I will," says Mam.

He sighs and grins, and stares past us like he can see right through the walls.

"I can see the sea, mates!" he says. "We're nearly there!"

And he falls asleep and starts to snore.

It smells of old bloke in here. Suppose it's bound to. Suppose he can't help it. Suppose I'll smell like old bloke myself one day. Pee and sweat and ancient clothes and dust. The sun shines through the window. Dust's glittering and dancing in the shafts of light. Outside there're the little trees in Harry's neat little garden, the rooftops of the street, Newcastle's towers and spires, then the big blue empty sky.

Mam lifts the papers out. She unfolds them from packets and envelopes while Harry snuffles and snores.

Here's his birth certificate.

Harold Matthew Miller

BORN:	*Nineteen Twenty-seven*
FATHER:	*Harold, a Turner*
MOTHER:	*Maisie, a Housewife*
ADDRESS:	*17 Blenkinsop Street, Newcastle-Upon-Tyne*

"Same address as now," I say.

"Aye. Lived here all his life. And look, this must be them."

It's a small faded black-and-white photograph. A young couple and a wrapped-up baby beaming through the years. Mam holds the photograph close to Harry's face. "Can you see them in him?" she says. And when we look at Harry and think of him with his wide and shining eyes, we have to say we can. The baby, the woman and the man are living on in the sleeping bloke.

More photographs: toddler Harry in a fat nappy with his dad in overalls on one side, Mam in a flowery frock on the other. Scruffy boys and girls on benches in an ancient schoolyard. A teacher at the centre with a big hooked nose and a fur wrap around her shoulders. Which one is he?

We pick the same face, the grinning kid just behind the teacher's head, the one lifting his hand like he wants to wave at us from seventy years ago. A final school report from 1942.

Harry is a fine hard-working lad. We wish him well in his chosen workplace.

There's his apprenticeship papers from the same year, when he started as an apprentice welder at Swan Hunter's shipyard. A photograph of him in a soldier's uniform. "National service," says Mam. Harry with girls, one pretty girl then another, then another. They're on Tynemouth seafront, on Newcastle quayside market, sitting in a Ferris wheel at a fair. There's a folded piece of pink paper with a handwritten note:

Thank you, Harry. Such a lovely day. Until next time. Love, V.

"V?" I say.

Mam shrugs.

"Who knows? I heard tell he'd been a ladies' man. Often chased but never caught."

She holds the photos to his face again.

"And there's still the handsome lad in him!" she says.

Then there he is in colour, in swimming trunks and with a sombrero on his head. He's linking arms with his mates on a beach in what Mam says must be Spain.

"That's Tommy Lind!" says Mam. "And Alex Marsh, God rest his soul."

There's more, and more. Photographs and documents,

savings books, rent books, pension books. There's his dad's death certificate in 1954, then his mother's just a few months later, both of them with cancer, both of them too young. There're holiday bookings, airline tickets, outdated foreign money. Lists of medication, prescriptions, hospital appointment cards.

"A whole life in a box," says Mam as she lifts another envelope and opens it. "What's this?" she says to herself.

"It's what I telt ye," says Harry. He's wide awake. "It's the Great North bliddy Run."

There're four skinny kids on a beach, three lads and a lass. The sun's blazing down. The lads are wearing baggy shorts and boots, and they've got vests slung over their bare shoulders. The lass is in a white dress and she's wearing boots as well. They're all grinning and holding massive ice creams in their fists.

"Pick us out," says Harry.

We both point to the same lad.

"That's reet," he says. "And that one's Norman Wilkinson, and he was Stanley Swift."

He pauses as he looks. He touches the girl's face and smiles. "She joined us at Felling. Veronica was her name."

He grins.

"It was took by Angelo Gabrieli, the ice-cream maker."

He keeps on grinning.

"It's South Shields," he says.

"South Shields?" says Mam.

"Look, there's the pier in the haze. There's Tynemouth Castle in the distance."

We peer closely.

"Oh, aye," we say.

"We run there from Newcastle," says Harry.

We just look at him.

"We were eleven years old," he says. "It was 1938. We were young and daft and fit as fleas."

He points to the envelope.

"Keep digging, hinny."

Mam takes out a sheet of paper. It crackles as she unfolds it. It's faded at the edges. The writing's all discoloured. She reads it out.

This is to sertify that
Harold Matthew Miller
run from Newcastle to South Shields on

29 August 1938

What a grate achievement!
Good lad! Well done!
Sined

Angelo Gabrieli

MASTER ICE-CREAM MAKER OF SOUTH SHIELDS,

29 AUGUST 1938

"He made one for all of us," says Harry. "And he sent the photographs to all of us."

We don't know what to say. He laughs at us.

"It's true," he says. "It was a lovely summer's day. Norman says, 'I'd love a swim.' So Stanley says, 'Let's go to Shields.'"

"But, Harry…" says Mam.

He points to the envelope.

"And we got our swim," he says.

Another photograph. The same kids, in the sea this time, yelling with laughter as the breakers roll over them.

"Beautiful," he murmurs. "We were that hot and sweaty and fit to drop, and it was wet and icy and tingly and just that lovely. And Mr Gabrieli with the camera. Can see him still, standing in the sunlight laughing and urging us on. Dark hair and dark eyes and broad shoulders and dressed in white. A lovely man."

"But it's thirteen miles," says Mam.

He sighs, he leans back in his chair. "Giz a minute. Any chance of a cup of tea?" She makes it. It trembles as he lifts it to his lips. He drinks. He drinks again. "Lovely cup of tea," he says. "One of them tablets. Aye, the white ones, love." He takes the tablet, he drinks more tea. He blinks, takes a breath. "Thirteen miles. We weren't to know. Stanley said he went there with his Uncle Jackie on the train one day. Said it was just across the Tyne Bridge then through a place called Felling then turn left and a short bit more. Said it'd mebbe take an hour at most and we'd be back for tea." He giggles.

"We didn't do geography at school, except to find out aboot Eskimos and pygmies and the River Nile."

"But what did you tell your mams?" says Mam.

"Nowt! Nowt at all." He looks at me. "We were always shooting off to the town moor or Exhibition Park, or just pottering around the streets and lanes. They were used to us going out in the morning and not

coming back till nearly dark. Don't believe it, de ye?"

"Dunno," I say.

"Different days, son. Mind you, by the time we got to Felling, we were starting to see what we'd took on."

He drinks some more tea.

"We started at ten o'clock. It was already hot. Stanley said, 'Just think of that icy watter on your skin, lads.'"

"So we belted out of Blenkinsop Street and down to the bridge. What a clatter! All of us had studs in our boots that our dads'd hammered in te mek them last

longer. We started off by racing each other, but after a while I said, 'Tek it easy, man, lads. No need for racing yet.'"

He looks at me. "You'll understand that, eh? Save some breath for the final sprint?"

"Aye, Mr Miller," I say.

"Aye. Good lad." He looks at my T-shirt again. "It's not the full run ye'll be diying, is it?"

"No," I say. "Just the junior one. A couple of miles around the bridges and the quay. You've got to be seventeen to do the proper Great North Run."

"Seventeen. So we were even dafter than I thought. Anyway, we trotted across the bridge and there were ships lined up along the river underneath, and seagulls screaming all around, and lots of folk walking on the bridge that we had to dodge past. We get to Gateshead and onto the High Street and we ask a fruiterer if we can have a drink of watter, please, cos we're running to South Shields today. 'To South bliddy Shields?' he says. 'You better have some apples an' all. Are ye sure?' he sez. 'Aye,' we say. 'It's just roond the corner, isn't it?' 'Depends what ye mean by roond the corner,' he says. We just laugh and take the apples and run on cos we're still full o' beans and it's great to be together on a summer's day. Then there's Sunderland Road that gets us to Felling, and it's a lang straight road and we've already been gannin' for nearly an hour. There's no sign of any sea, no end in sight.

"And we sit doon by Felling railway station and we look at each other and nobody says a word till Norman says at last, 'So where the hell's South Shields?' Stanley points along the road. 'That way, I think,' he says. 'I divent knaa exactly, but I'm certain we're gannin' the reet way.' Norman just looks at him. 'I'm getting knackered,' he says. 'Let's gan back.' And probly we would have. But then we seen her, across the street, lookin' doon at us."

"Who?" says Mam.

"Veronica."

He sips his tea again. He sighs and blows.

"You knaa," he says. "It comes to something when talking aboot runnin' gets as knackerin' as runnin' itself." He grins. "Divent get old, son. Promise us that. Stay eleven for ever."

"OK, Mr Miller," I say.

"Good lad. I bet you're fast, are ye?"

"Not that fast. I can keep going, though."

"Ye'd have been good that day, then. And ye'll be all set when you're seventeen."

"Aye. I think I will."

"Just wait till ye see that sea, shining before ye after all them miles."

"Veronica, Harry," says Mam.

"Eh?" says Harry.

"Veronica. Who was she?"

"Veronica? She was something else."

He turns his face to the ceiling. He closes his eyes like he's imagining it all again, then he opens them again and there's such a smile on his face.

"She was on the green at the end of a row of terraced houses," he says. "She was hanging washing oot. She stopped what she was diyin' and she had one hand up across her eyes to shade them from the sun. 'Gan and ask her for some watter,' sez Norman. 'Gan yourself,' sez Stanley. 'I'll gan,' sez I. And off I go. I can see her now, standing in her white cotton dress with the basket of washing under her arm and the way she watches us as I get closer.

"'What do you want?' she sez. 'Is there any chance of a cup of watter?' I say. 'We've been runnin' from Newcastle and we're parched.' 'From Newcastle?' she sez. 'Aye,' I say. 'From Blenkinsop Street. We were ganna run te South Shields but I think we're turning back.' 'Why's that?' she sez. 'Cos we're knackered,' I say. 'And South Shields is a lang way. And to be honest we divent really knaa where it is.' She puts the washing doon. 'Turning back?' she sez. 'And you don't even know where it is? What kind of attitude is that?' 'I divent knaa,' I say. 'But if you'll be kind enough to give us some watter we'll be on our way.' And she sez, 'Wait there,' and she turns round and walks away."

Harry says nothing for a while. It looks like he's going all dreamy again, like he might doze off again.

"Did she bring some water?" says Mam.

"Eh? Aye, she did. A big bottle of it. And she's got jam sandwiches an' all, and she's got big boots on and she sez, 'There's no need to turn back. I know where South Shields is. I've left a note for my mother. I'll take you there.' And she puts a sandwich in me hand, and walks down to where the other two is. She tells them an' all

while they're eating the sandwiches and swigging the watter. 'But we're half knackered already,' sez Stanley. 'By the time we run aal the way back again we'll be bliddy deed.' 'There's no need to run back again,' she sez. 'We can take the train. You'll be back for tea.' And when we start to laugh she goes into the pocket in her dress and takes some money out. 'I'll pay,' she sez. 'My Uncle Donald sends it to me. He lives in America. He says he works in Hollywood. I think he's fibbing

but that doesn't matter.' Me and the lads look at each other. A train steams through the station. I look at her, I think of the train, I taste the lovely bread and jam, and I swig the lovely watter. 'I'm Veronica,' says Veronica. 'What're your names?' So we tell her, and so she says, 'What we waiting for?' She smiles her smile at me. Me and the lads look at each other. 'Nowt,' I say. 'Nowt,' say the other two. 'This way, then,' she sez, and we set off running again."

"Quite a girl," says Mam.
"Aye," says Harry.

He goes silent again. Mam says does he want more tea. He says yes. She goes to make it. I look at my watch, I think about Jacksie, I think about running through Jesmond Dene.

"Things to do?" says Harry.

"Aye."

He nods. "I'll not be lang. I cannot be. Or like Stanley said, by the time I finish I'll be bliddy dead. More tea. Good lass! Ha, and a slice of jam and bread and all!"

Mam smiles with him.

"Eat it up," she says. "It'll give you strength."

And he eats, and wipes his lips with his shaky hand, and after a moment he starts again.

"So we run out of Felling and down through Pelaw and Bill Quay and into Hebburn, and it's getting hot as Hell and staying bright as Heaven. And Veronica runs smooth and free beside us. And our feet clatter and beat on the tracks and pavements, and sometimes we walk and rest and gather our breath and run again.

And sometimes we shout out to folks we pass that we're running to South Shields and we've run from Blenkinsop Street in Newcastle and from Felling station and they say they don't believe it. They say it's such a bliddy wonder! 'Good lads!' they say. 'Good lass! Run! Run! There's a wolf at your tail! Run for your lives!' And people give us watter, and a baker in Hebburn gives us cakes. And we run and run and run and run.

"And we get to Jarrow and we rest in the shade under the trees in St John's churchyard, and we watch a coffin bein' carried from a hearse through a group of mourners and put into the ground, and out of the blue Veronica stretches her arms out wide and says, 'They said I might not live at all. And just look what I can do!'"

"How do you mean?" says Mam.

"That's what I sez – 'How d'you mean?' Veronica shrugs. 'I was a weakly child,' she says. 'I was back and forward to the doors of death.' Me and the lads is hushed. They were different days back then. There were many little'ns took too soon. Stanley hisself had a sister gone before he was born. 'Are you all right now?' he whispers to Veronica. And she laughs, the way she did. 'Now how could I run to South Shields if I wasn't, Stanley?' And up she jumps with her big heart and her big soul and her strong legs and her big boots and we're off again, and as we leave Jarrow behind we start telling each other we can smell the sea. Which was more a matter of hope than truth. Nae sign of any sea.

Nae sign of any South Shields. We've soon been gone more than two hours. It's afternoon. It's blazin' hot. We're absolutely knacked. We're slowin' doon. Nobody says it but we're all thinking of giving up. Even Veronica starts puffin' and pantin' and gaspin' for air, and Stanley's watching her with great concern. And then we hear it, the clip-clop-clip of Gabrieli's pony and the toot of Gabrieli's horn." He laughs at the memory. "It come upon us like a miracle."

"The ice-cream maker?" says Mam.

"Aye. Mr Angelo Gabrieli, master ice-cream maker of South Shields. He's on an ice-cream cart that's painted

all white and red and gold. The pony's shining black. Mr
Gabrieli's sitting there in his white shirt and his white
trousers and his white cap with **GABRIELI'S** printed on
it and there's a great big tub of ice cream at his side.
He toots his horn again. He laughs. 'Buy a Gabrieli!' he
calls. 'Best ice cream this side of Heaven!' And he tugs
the pony to a halt at our side. We halt as well. We puff
and pant. We drool. We watch the shining tub. I think of
Veronica's cash. Never mind the train, I think. Buy some
ice creams now! 'Good afternoon, my fine children!'
says Mr Gabrieli. 'And where might you be going on
this perfect day?' 'South Shields,' I tell him. He grins in

satisfaction. 'The perfect destination! Your names, my friends?' We tell him our names. I tell him we've run all the way from Newcastle and Felling. 'Indeed?' he says. 'I thought you looked a little hot. Perhaps a little ice cream would be rather helpful.' We daren't speak. We look at Veronica. Our eyes and hearts are yearning. 'Perhaps a little one now,' says Mr Gabrieli, 'and the biggest one you've ever seen when at last you reach the beach!' And he opens the tub and digs into it, and gives us each an

ice cream for free. Ha! And nothing I've tasted in the seventy years since has tasted anything like that glorious gift. Mr Gabrieli smiles as he watches us. He ponders. 'I could offer you a lift,' he says and Norman's mouth is opening wide with joy. But Veronica's shaking her head and telling him no. 'Yes, you are right, Veronica,' says Mr Gabrieli. 'This is an achievement you will remember all your lives. Do not worry, boys. It is not far now. Along here then right and onto lovely Ocean Road, and then at the end of that – the shining sea itself! I will meet you there!' He snaps the reins. 'Onward, Francisco! Until we meet again, my friends!' And off he trots."

Harry rests. He gazes out at the trees and the sky. Mam brings more tea.

"You've not told anybody about this till now?" she says.

"I've told bits of it, pet, just like bits of crack and reminiscing at the club. But I've never telt it all with all the detail in. And even now, there'll be bits of it I must leave out."

"It was such an amazing thing, Harry," Mam says.

"Like Mr Gabrieli said, such a great achievement."

"Aye, that's true. And it was a day of daftness and joy, and if we'd never started and we'd never kept on going, just think of what we'd've missed." He smiles, like he's slipping into a dream. "So we kept on going and we kept on going. We followed Gabrieli's cart until it went right out of sight, and we kept on going with the lovely thought of massive ice creams still to come. And then we're on Ocean Road, and there's seagulls in the air and a breeze on our faces, and this time we can truly smell the sea, and then, 'Oh, I can see it, mates! I can really see the sea!'"

And Harry's eyes are wide, like he can see the sea again.

"And he's there, like he said he would be. Mr Gabrieli. He's sitting up on his cart and he smiles to welcome us and holds his arms out wide. 'Now,' he says. 'Which should come first? The ice cream or the sea?' And we divent hesitate.

"We're straight onto the beach and plunging into the watter. And when we look back, there's Mr Gabrieli laughing at us as we jump and dive and tumble through the waves.

"Then we stand together and he photographs us, and we come out and he leads us to the cart and he gives us the biggest ice creams we've ever seen, then he photographs us again. And he has our certificates ready and we sit in the sand and read them to each other. And then Mr Gabrieli asks us if we know that we are wonderful, and he sings to us – something I never heard before and have never heard since, except in dreams, something Italian and strange and very beautiful."

He points to the envelope.

"Should be something else in there," he says. "He got some passer-by to take it."

Mam slips her fingers inside and takes it out, another photograph. Everybody's in it, standing smiling before the ice-cream cart and Francisco the shining pony. Harry, Veronica, Stanley and Norman with their certificates, and lovely Mr Gabrieli himself, all in white with **GABRIELI'S** printed on his cap, and past them is the beach and then the sea. And me and Mam don't say anything, though we can see that Harry and Veronica are standing right together, holding hands.

"And then," says Harry, "we give our addresses to Mr Gabrieli and we say goodbye. And back we go up Ocean Road and to the railway station. And then we get the train, and off it puffs, through Jarrow and Hebburn and Pelaw and Heworth, doing in minutes what took us so long. And then along the track to Felling."

"And Veronica?" says Mam.

"She got off there. And we went on. And we were home in time for tea."

"You know what I mean. Did you see her again?"

"Most nights, in me dreams."

"No more than that?"

He shakes his head, closes his eyes, then points into the box.

"That brown packet there," he says.

She lifts it out.

"Gan on," he says.

She opens it, and there they are, Harry and Veronica. They're on the Tyne Bridge, maybe eighteen years old. The breeze is in their hair and there're seagulls in the air behind them, and they're laughing out loud and holding hands again.

"Aye," he says. He takes the photograph and holds it. "We made sure we found each other again. And we were together for a time. And she really was something else. But then…"

His voice falters. He shakes his head.

"Not now, love. I'm knacked. The lad's got running to do, I've got a home to go to, and you've got some helping out to do."

"OK then, Harry," says Mam.

She kisses him. She tells him to close his eyes, to have a rest.

"Aye, I will," he says. He licks his lips and stares into the photograph.

"Do you think…?" he says to Mam.

"Think what, Harry?"

"Do you think there's a Heaven, like they used to say there was? A Heaven where we meet again?"

"I don't know, Harry."

"Me neither. And mebbe it doesn't matter. Mebbe this is Heaven. Mebbe you enter Heaven on the best of days, like the day we got to Shields, like other days."

"Days with her? With Veronica?"

"Aye. Days with Veronica."

His eyes flutter. He looks at me.

"You're a good lad. Get started, keep on going. You'll have a lovely life."

He closes his eyes.

"You know what?" he murmurs before he sleeps. "Me great achievement is that I've been happy, that I've never been nowt but happy."

"Go on, son," says Mam. "Go and see Jacksie. Get your training in."

Harry never got to St Mary's Nursing Home. He died that afternoon while I was running with Jacksie through Jesmond Dene. Mam said he just slipped away like he was going into a deeper sleep. She arranged the funeral. People came to our house afterwards. We played a CD of Italian songs. There was beer and a big tub of ice cream, and there was crying, and lots and lots of laughter. I ran again that afternoon with Jacksie, and I heard Harry deep inside me: "That's reet, lad! Run! There's a wolf at your tail! Run for your lovely life!"

A week later we ran the Junior Great North Run. We belted round the quayside and across the bridges, hundreds of us running through the sunlight by the glittering river and through the cheering crowds. We raced each other to the finish line, me an' my best mate Jacksie, numbers 2593 and 2594, and Jacksie just got there in front of me. It didn't matter. We stood arm in arm with our medals and certificates. We laughed into Mam's camera. We were young and daft. We'd run the run, and we felt so free and light I really thought we might have run into a bit of Heaven.

Next day Mam drove us all to Felling. We stood on the bypass and here they came, the thin, fast lines of professionals and champions and record-holders and harriers; then the others – hundreds after hundreds after hundreds of them – puffing and panting, grinning

and gasping. Here came the young and the old, the determined and the barmy. They waved and grimaced and sighed and giggled. They squirted water over their heads and over us. There were gorillas and ducks and Supermen and bishops and Frankensteins and Draculas and nurses. And the watchers laughed and yelled.

"You're doing great!" yelled Mam. "Good lad! Good lass! Gan on! Well done!"

And then I saw them. They were kids, too little and young for this run. Three skinny lads in vests and boots that thudded on the road, a fair-haired lass in boots as well and wearing a white dress. They twisted and dodged and threaded their way through the crowd.

And I looked at Mam a moment, and her eyes were wide with astonishment and wonder as well. As the four of them passed by, one of the lads lifted his hand high and waved at us and laughed, and then was off again. And they'd gone, lost again in the crowd, a crowd that kept on running past and running past, a crowd we couldn't wait to join, a crowd that seemed like the whole of Tyneside, the whole of the world, all running through the blazing sunlight to the sea.